A Friend Like Him

Written by SUZANNE FRANCIS

Illustrated by DOMINIC CAROLA AND RYAN FELTMAN

FOR JACK

—S. F.

TO GOOD FRIENDS THAT I'VE BEEN HONORED
TO WORK AND SHARE LIFE WITH

—D. C.

TO MY LOVING WIFE FOR ALL HER SUPPORT,
ALLOWING ME TO LIVE MY DREAM
AS A PROFESSIONAL ARTIST

—R. F.

Printed in the United States of America

First Hardcover Edition, April 2019

3   5   7   9   10   8   6   4   2

ISBN 978-1-368-03707-5

Library of Congress Control Number: 2018955546

FAC-034274-19176

Designed by Soyoung Kim

For more Disney Press fun, visit www.disneybooks.com

This is the genie.

Everyone calls him . . .

GENIE.

He spends LOADS of time inside his teeny-tiny home,
which happens to be a lamp.

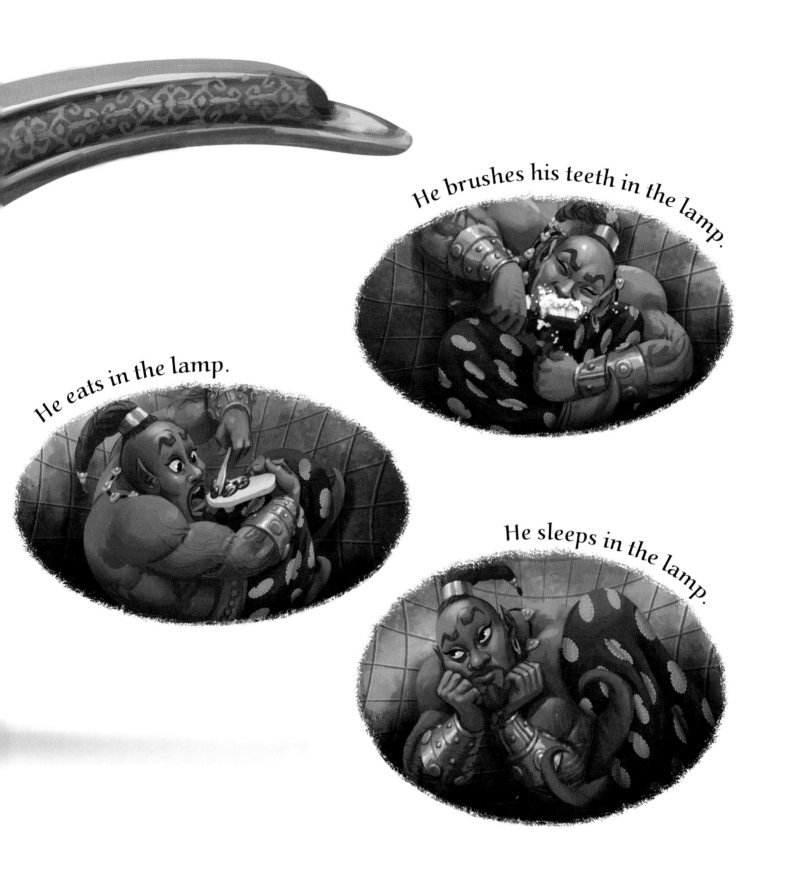

He brushes his teeth in the lamp.

He eats in the lamp.

He sleeps in the lamp.

But more than anything else, he stares at
lots and lots of brass. It gets pretty boring and lonely.

Genie only comes OUT of the lamp if somebody finds it.
And that is quite a task, because it's usually buried in some deep,
dark, scary place . . . like a magical cave in the middle of the desert.

Most of the people who find Genie's lamp spend years and years and years looking for it.

ONE GUY SEARCHED HIS ENTIRE LIFE!

When somebody does find the lamp,
they rub it and . . .

POOF!

Out Genie comes.

Then they can ask for THREE WISHES.
Genie uses his magic to grant each one.

Lots of the people who find Genie's lamp have a certain look in their eyes. They know exactly what they want . . . and it's usually money, power, or fame.

LIKE THIS GUY.

AND THIS GUY.

Every few hundred years or so,
there is someone who finds the lamp accidentally.

LIKE THIS CAMEL.

AND THIS BABY.

But one day a very different kind of person found Genie's lamp.
His name was ALADDIN. He went into the deep, dark, dangerous
magical cave because a man —much like the others—had tricked him.

Aladdin didn't know anything about Genie or his magic.
But when he rubbed some dirt off the side of the lamp . . .

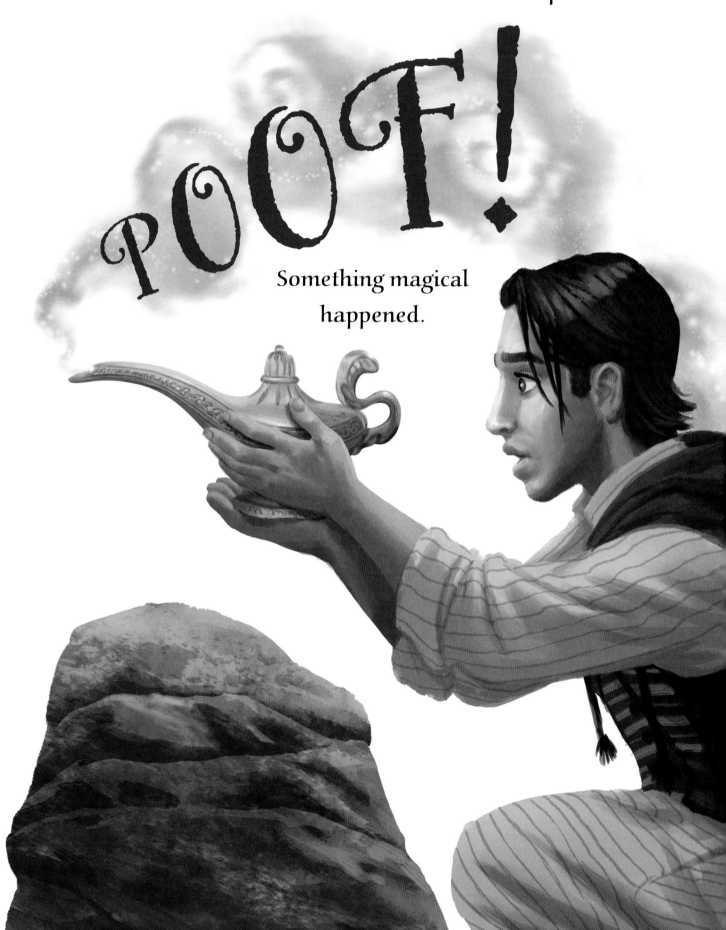

POOF!

Something magical
happened.

Genie emerged.
Aladdin had never seen anything like that before.
He thought Genie was a giant. He had never even heard of genies!

Genie could tell right away that Aladdin was different. He didn't have that creepy look in his eyes, and he asked how long Genie had been inside the lamp. Genie was happy to answer:

"'BOUT A THOUSAND YEARS."

Aladdin was amazed . . . and still very confused.

Genie was more than happy to demonstrate his incredible skills.

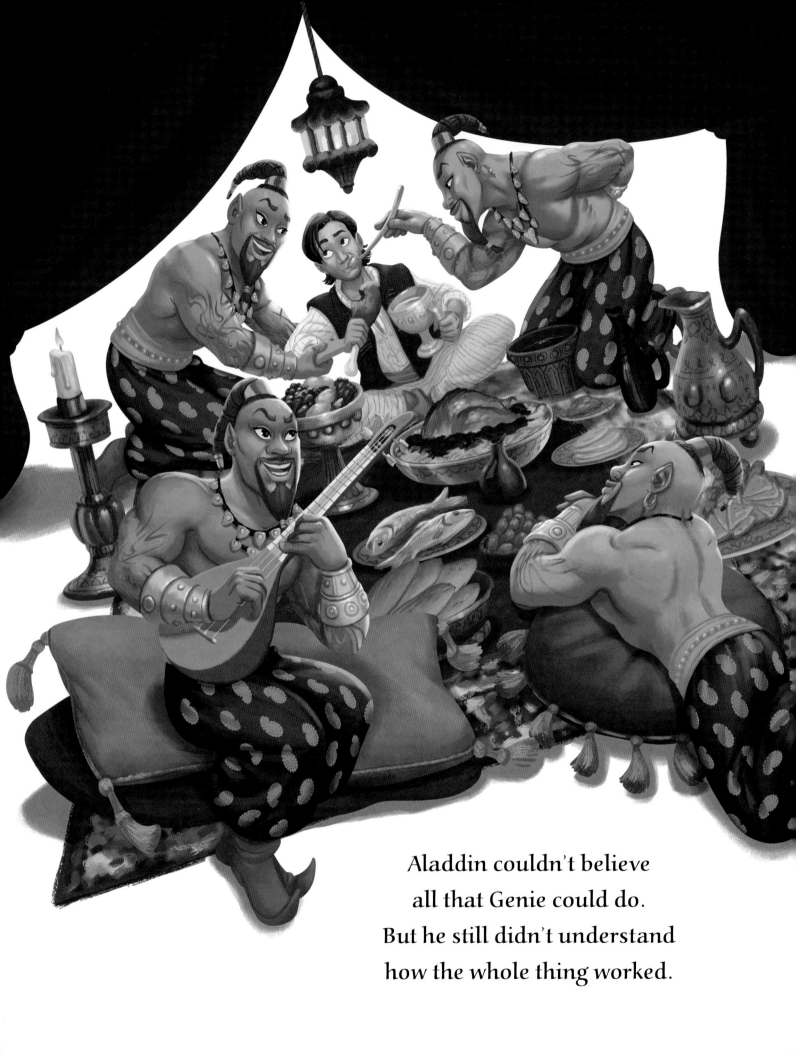

Aladdin couldn't believe
all that Genie could do.
But he still didn't understand
how the whole thing worked.

Genie explained. "You have three wishes,
and they must begin with rubbing the lamp and saying:

'I WISH.' GOT IT?"

RUB THE LAMP

SAY WHAT YOU WANT

THERE IS NO STEP 3!

Aladdin nodded. Then Genie pointed out some basic rules.

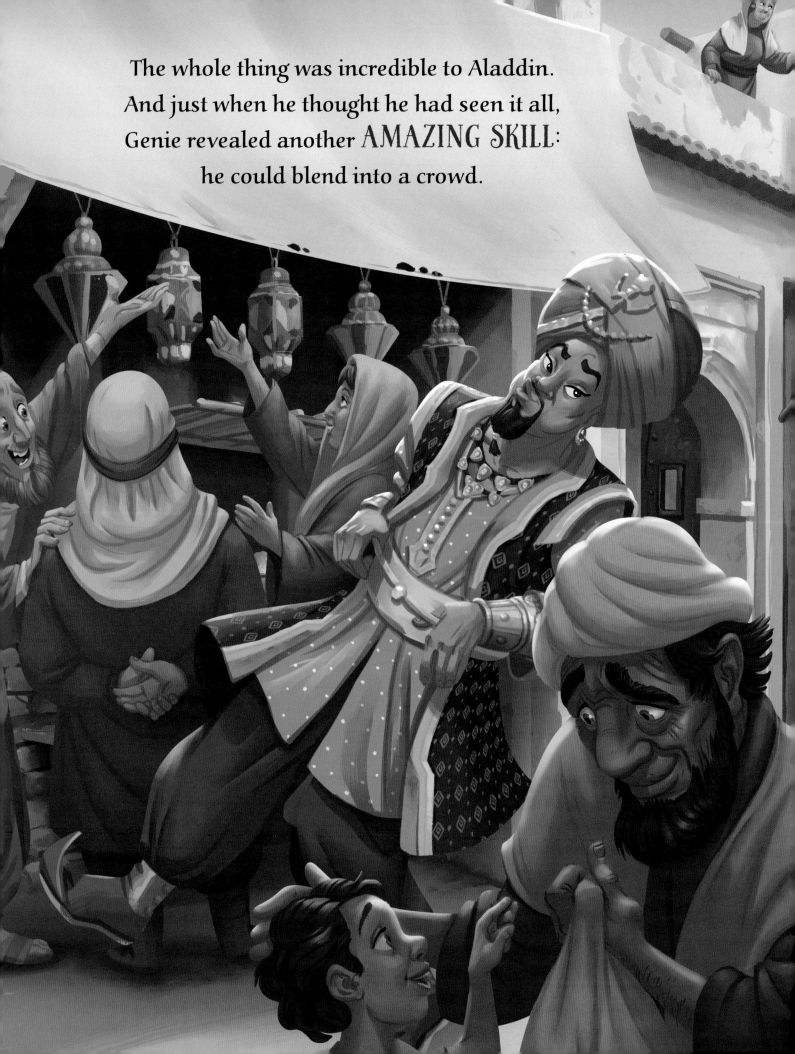

The whole thing was incredible to Aladdin.
And just when he thought he had seen it all,
Genie revealed another AMAZING SKILL:
he could blend into a crowd.

Aladdin liked Genie. He thought they could be friends,
but Genie explained that genies didn't really have friends.
Of course, people wanted Genie to be THEIR
friend because of all the great things he could give them.
That wasn't a TRUE FRIENDSHIP.

But Genie kind of liked Aladdin, so he also told him
how important it was to correctly word a wish.
"Use your words—avoid sticky misunderstandings," he said.

He explained how one guy's wish to be
"MOST ATTRACTIVE"
turned him into a human magnet.

Another's wish to be
"RICH AND HANDSOME"
landed him a new name.

Birth Certificate:
Richard
N.
Handsome

And when someone else said,
"MAKE ME A PRINCE,"
he ended up with a little royal
dude following him around.

When Aladdin asked Genie what he would wish for,
Genie was stunned. "Wow . . . nobody's ever asked me
that before. But that's easy." Genie's wish was to live outside
the lamp and never have to grant another wish again!

Aladdin wanted to impress Princess Jasmine.
After giving it some thought, he said,

"I WISH TO BECOME
A PRINCE."

Hearing Aladdin's perfectly worded wish, Genie nodded
proudly. He could tell Aladdin had been listening.

With some big Genie magic . . .

BOOM!

Aladdin became Prince Ali of Ababwa.

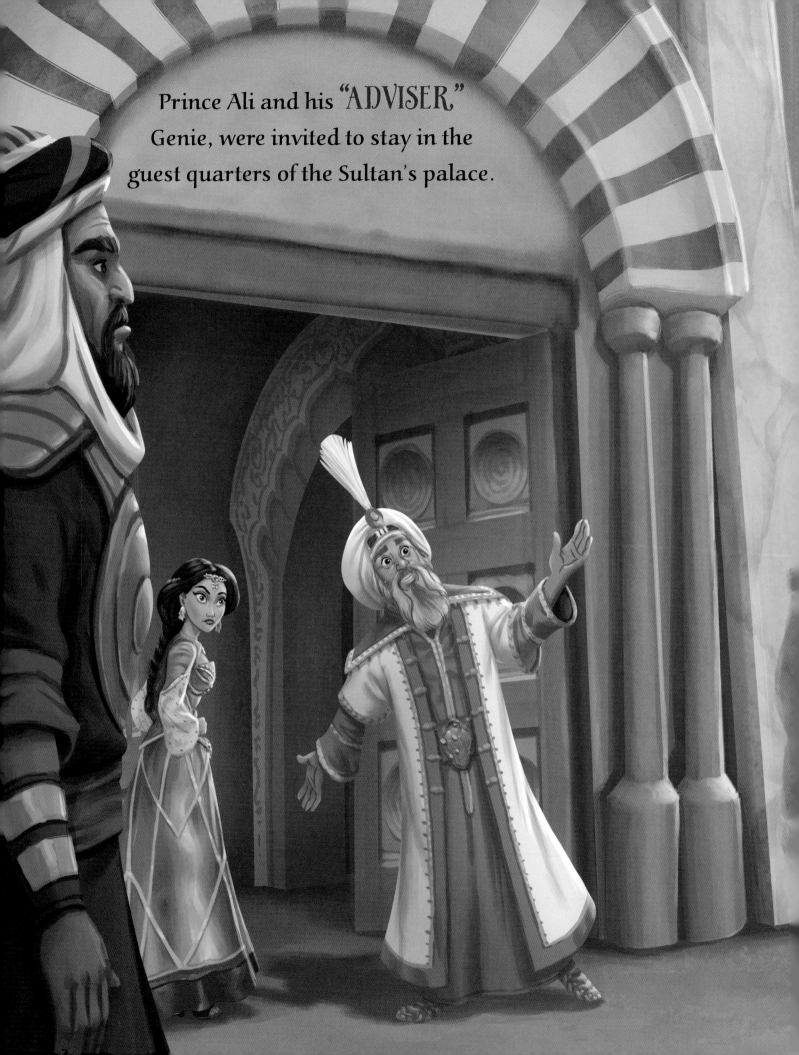

Prince Ali and his "ADVISER,"
Genie, were invited to stay in the
guest quarters of the Sultan's palace.

Aladdin was nervous around Princess Jasmine,
so Genie helped him work on his confidence.

Genie and Aladdin spent
a lot of time together,
having fun and watching
out for each other.

When Aladdin nearly drowned,
Genie didn't hesitate to help him.

Aladdin was grateful to Genie for saving his life.
"THANK YOU, GENIE," he said.

Genie was HAPPY that Aladdin was okay, and to his surprise,
he realized . . . HE REALLY CARED ABOUT ALADDIN.

Aladdin surprised Genie again when he made
his final wish. It wasn't for himself, but for

HIS GOOD FRIEND GENIE.

Aladdin and Genie both knew they had gotten
something even a powerful genie couldn't grant:

A TRUE FRIEND.